Catharsis

Evincepub
Publishing

Evincepub Publishing

Parijat Extension, Bilaspur, Chhattisgarh 495001

First Published by Evincepub Publishing 2018
Copyright © Chinmay Kar 2018
All Rights Reserved.
ISBN: 978-93-87905-90-0
Price: Rs.180/-

CATHARSIS

A TALE OF IMPERFECT COINCIDENCES

MAYBE IT'S HOW YOU GROW UP, NOT WHEN

Chinmay Kar

iv

ABOUT THE AUTHOR

Chinmay divyadarshi Kar, the Author is a 20-year-old student currently pursuing his MBBS career in Institute of Medical Sciences and SUM hospital under Siksha 'O' Anusandhan (SOA) University, Bhubaneswar. Being newly gifted with his skills of writing, he is still under a process of development on making his best self to come out to reflect upon his career. Apart from writing he also holds interest on the mysteries of the human brain function and its response on various changes occurring in our day to day lives, believes on a day when every human in planet would understand the true value of emotions. Apart from this he also enjoys Speed thrill, Computer games, Japanese music, reading novels. Becoming a successful doctor is one of his dreams yet to achieve and make perfect.

ABOUT THE BOOK

This book contains a story of an adult who has entered his early twenties. This late teenage, early adulthood is a phase where they have it all: youth, energy, health, and looks. But they are also filled with life transitions from childhood to adulthood that can be stressful. Hence this book generally focuses on the flash thoughts which generally occurs during this age by revolving around the story of a man who started his day with a perfectly planned routine life but eventually comes across the hardships and the tough decisions which everyone in their life story have to eventually go through. It is the coincidences which he faced in just 24 hours which helped him to recalibrate his mind and emerge from his cocoon to become a matured adult who was once a smart man. Be a part of this short yet epic thrilling adventure of Charan and behold as he makes amends with his past to emerge victorious and matured.

This book is dedicated to the negative thoughts of mine whom I have purged.

ACKNOWLEDGEMENTS

The book which you are currently holding in your palm and have shown a keen interest to read is the result of all those who have been a part of my journey which led me to attain catharsis.

First of all, I am very grateful to the Almighty who has gifted me this ability of expressing my thoughts through words for which I will forever be obliged.

My father Dr Chittaranjan Kar, mother Sumita Mishra and my brother Pankaj Priyadarshi Kar have encouraged me to maintain my homeostasis even in the toughest and the darkest times of all and helped me believe that failure is a choice and never permanent. So any amount of acknowledgment to them would not suffice for such a wonderful upbringing.

I would also like to thank my friends and colleagues who have supported me and encouraged me to write further at times when writing a poem was just another hobby among a couple others. Had it not been so, this whole book would have just drifted away in my thoughts.

Lot of thanks to my Author friend, colleague and a brother through emotions, Rahul Kanungo who supported me at all times and led my mind to this enlightened path of self-understanding through his book "Reconciliation: Rhythms from the twenty first century" and many more books coming in future.

I also appreciate the efforts made by my publishing team Evincepub who by their tireless efforts have made this book a reality in a very short course of time and have turned my thoughts into an accredited paperwork.

Here is cheers to all those people who have guided me to see life through different perceptions. This book is for all those well-wishers.

CONTENTS

THE HARSH REALITY

This book revolves around the story of a boy who has entered his early twenties. This late teenage, early adulthood is a phase where they have it all: youth, energy, health and looks. But they are also still figuring themselves out, and this time of change can bring certain mental health concerns as well. The twenties are an important time of social/emotional development and are filled with life transitions that can be stressful as the young adults are solidifying their personalities, developing their independence from family, starting or finishing college, beginning new jobs, developing a career, making new relationships and learning to manage their existing family relationships and friendships within these contexts.

These individuals don't have a lifetime experience to draw on when managing multiple life transitions simultaneously. When someone experiences these transitions, anxiety and depressive disorders can occur. Unlike previous generations, identity formation often takes the entire twenties due to the complexity of modern society.

During this phase of development, adolescents enter a transition from childhood to adulthood. Issues of independence, identity, sexuality and relationships define this developmental stage. Mental health problems, such as mood disorders, anxiety disorders and thought disorders (like schizophrenia) as well as psychosocial disorders, may develop or become apparent during this stage. Suicide is a leading cause of death for this age group.

Hence, this book generally focuses on the flash thoughts which predominantly occurs during this age by revolving around a story of a man who started his day with a perfectly planned routine life but eventually comes across the hardships and the tough decisions which everyone in their life story have to eventually go through. It is the co-incidences which he faced in just 24 hours which helped him to recalibrate his mind and emerge from his cocoon in order to become a mature adult who was once a smart man. Be a part of this short yet epic thrilling adventure of Charan and behold as he makes amends with his past to emerge as victorious and mature.

Remember, one gets mature only when he makes amends and reconciles with his Past. When your heart and mind synchronise, then only one becomes unstoppable.

IMPERFECT COINCIDENCES

It was the day of the month of fewest daylight hours. With the ringing sound of alarm clock stuck at 5, a young boy woke up rubbing his eyes with an iced cupid bow. Wintery chills sneaked into the room as he stretched himself and prepared for the day. Though he was living alone, still there was no evidence of any mess. A blue sweat shirt hung up on his hanger with yellow bold letters in the back revealing the name "CHARAN".

He watched the sea coast and how the sun rise looked from his porch. He chuckled after looking at the sun peeping out like a baby from the bed sheet of ocean-green sea. Sound of sweeping dust was heard as he gazed down to the lady holding a broom of half her size and coughing out smog.

It wasn't too long for him to get ready for his jogging. The month of extreme cold embraced the whole town with the chills. But Charan was a dreamy boy who would never miss his one time of day appreciating the vastness of the beauty. Every morning he would dedicate his thoughts on the peculiarity of life and how it can be compared with an example of a day. A regular **THOUGHTFUL MORNING** is what he would say that to himself.

Chinmay Kar

THOUGHTFUL MORNING

What to say? It was a casual Monday morning blues
Woke up in bed feeling being inside a cruise.

As wintery morning, I felt the cold morning breeze
Well it was enough to get me stand freeze.

Literally the darkness lifted before my eyes
Wasn't the first time, but got me thinking while looking
at skies.

Isn't the cycle of morning, noon and night similar to
life?
Some say existence's a thing tough to describe.

But according to me, it's as simple as a day
Morning marks childhood when we used to only play.

Then comes noon bringing maximum pain overhead
Signifies adult, getting zealous to get rewarded.

And after showing that diligences, we finally grow
senile
Like night spreading its cold coat saying it's still agile.

Now the deep essence of this morning thought is
There's many things in life to get replenished.

Depends on how you choose to remember every moment
To see that inspiration, doesn't demand being brilliant.

Sometimes you have to close your eyes to actually see
As those who have mastered it are the ones calling
themselves free.

Besides appreciating the vastness of beauty, he would also observe and analyse other peoples who have been kept as the prisoners of themselves.

People howling over the bus, pushing each other hard only to grab a seat and their precious gadgets sitting like a crowned king on its master's lap, while their children are crying for closure.

Busy with doing serious jobs is what they would tell to everyone but Charan is also a successful grad student who excels in academics as well as relationships, and he doesn't consider all these as obstacles who would come in between a son and mother that is "His motherland/*matrubhumi*".

Often he ponders over the glory of the earth on which he stands and with how many struggles in the past has been faced by his mother to safeguard her children. Bow and Salute to this mother **FROM A CARING SON**.

—————◆—————

FROM A CARING SON

So the day has just began
Everyone's getting busy, No time to even stand.

But am I the only one to see
To think about our motherland, no one's ever free.

How naive, even I got the thought quite late
Not judging but ask yourself, is this our fate.

This mother has taken care of our whole generation
Many tried to break her, she still stands giving
inspiration.

She is the mother of all Sons, Daughters, Fathers and
Mothers
Teaching us from start to chase dreams without feathers.

Because in order to rise, one must first learn to fall
That's how success lets us stand tall.

So if we have time to put stories/Selfies in Facebook and
Insta
Why not also put a picture of Mother India.

Chinmay Kar

Now some may say am getting over patronised
But doing a bit for nation, don't you feel satisfied?

While I wrote this, Sun rose to start the day
So at last I would just like to say.

The worlds changing doesn't mean you also have to
change
We think less about things that really matter, isn't it
strange?

Charan was just returning to his flat when his phone buzzed with a text saying "Morning!". With a grin in his face, he wiped up his sweat as it was the text from a friend named 'PRIYA' whom he had recently befriended. Not sure what his relationship is but he would often text her informing about the situations he faces and would find comfort to summarise his day to her, though it was not mutual. For Priya, it was just getting to know each other and nothing more.

Most of the time, Charan would skip his meals or routine assignments only to spend time with her when she would feel depressed or lonely. He also finds comfort when he successfully manages to make Priya laugh even in difficult times, but also feels fatigued after sacrificing his sleep to makeover his skipped routines.

After talking with Priya while jogging, he returned to his flat, changed his clothes, groomed himself and carried his backpack as he rode to his hospital in his car where he works as a junior resident aspiring to be a great surgeon one day.

While driving too he doesn't miss out to have some fun as he lowers his side window and gulps all the fresh hair as he **TRAVELS LIFE**.

Chinmay Kar

TRAVELLING LIFE

Life is just like travelling a road
At some point, it's natural to get bored.

It's up to us what we would like to fill it with
Because that's what we will be getting at the end of it.

Some travel the road with pain and agony
While some make peace and remain jolly.

There will be ups and downs of it no doubt
Depends on what we are making from that out.

Either we fright and choose the sideway
Or become brave and go on highway.

Whether by seeing an obstacle we stop the car
Or smash through it to reach far.

There will be things destroying the road like showering
rain
What to do? Let it continue or wipe the water to drain.

Depends on how you choose to see your life
Nevertheless always try hard to make it thrive.

Those who respect life, no one can snatch their success
So always try to spread Positiveness
Fill the road with chips of happiness
Prove your life's worthiness
Overcome the void and fill the damn emptiness.

There was a look of responsible young man with a pair of jet black pupils under bushy eyebrows as he marched to the building of white walls wearing a white coat filled with coloured post it notes in its pockets accompanied by marker pens.

He takes pride carrying around his stethoscope on his shoulder which he has earned through his hardships in medical school. Through his well-versed knowledge, his friends would often like to take his suggestion on how much dose to administer or how to manage a complicated case. He takes pride when he hears his name to be called as a bookworm or a nerd.

Colleagues would often test him by putting him in a hypothetical situation and how he would proceed. Being a dedicated friend, he would spill every bit of information churning his brain but his "mates" would often take the credit of his information and would still underrate him in front of his mentors. Though it would sometimes hurt him, still he wouldn't find the reason to be that big to make an issue.

For him, friends are like the clones of himself which he should never get hold off. It's better to live in happiness with **FRIENDS** than pitying with loneliness.

<u>FRIENDS</u>

Everyone has a friend in their life
Being with them, we often lose time

They are the spitting image of us
A sibling whom we can endlessly trust

Earlier, hanging out was the job of parents
Now they have got replaced with friends

With them, fun is the only thing that happens
Well, it's much better than suffering from loneliness

The friends come in different variety
Combine us and ensure lethality

Dumb or smart, it doesn't matter
Happiness is the only thing we scatter

Sad or lonely; their presence makes us smile
God! May we always be like a chime

We learn new things; facts by them to survive
Pseudo friend is the only thing one can never derive

People say "We pray god; what do we get"
It's God which gives friends as a pleasure to taste

They act as antacids to eradicate seriousness
Compromise is the thing we learn for togetherness

So, at last a lonely would ask "What did I get"
But a lucky one will just have a laugh in death bed.

With his friends sharing his dream of being a surgeon, he often would go to the dissection hall to brush up his Anatomy.

While cutting the dead flesh, he chuckles as the memories of his first year in med school rushed in his brains with a flash. The smell of the cadaver, the contents of dissection box containing scissor, forceps, scalpels and dipping the hands in formalin and later smelling it throughout the day.... He remembered it all as he perfected his technique of "chop and stop" to cut the fat layers.

With a room full of dead bodies, he would never fear but would sometimes get surprised when a breeze of cold wind would slash itself on his warm skin making its way through the pores of his linen shirt. A beautiful scenery of mountain filled with gigantic trees was another reason luring him into the chamber of cold flesh.

Although he has byhearted all the structures down to its cell morphology, he still gets amazed with the subject named **ANATOMY**.

Chinmay Kar

AMAZING ANATOMY

In medical college, there is a subject named Anatomy
This subject teaches us about human morphology.

First thing in lab we see is a cadaver
We pull out everything… kidney, heart or liver

This smell of cadaver teaches us patience
Students plan to tackle smells resistance.

The passion of dissecting overcomes all joy
Once stepped in those waters, you are not that same
girl/boy.

Massive respect to ones who donate their body
Help students to forge their careers first story.

Everyone carries dissection box for dissecting
A jolt is felt when hands are dipped in formalin.

Overall it's a subject where we learn to play with
scissors and scalpel
Though learning all, the origin and insertion of muscles
is such a hell.

Oh! The scarcity of books during our tests
Standing outside hall with piles of sweat and wishing all
the best.

After cutting through his adventures, he rushes to attend his lectures. Though it brushes up the knowledge, Charan finds it boring and yawns like a grizzly bear having a mouth full of his preys. He slacks off on writing the lecture notes. Instead finds to look around and what others are doing as a better option.

Well you can never expect someone to be that perfect and studious, sometimes it's better to slack off and take a dedicated nap, but taking a nap during lecture means walking on fire as well as on water at the same time. He can never do that, so he tries to talk with others but realises no one really cares to talk to him instead of fooling around in smartphones.

He finds another solution of making his mind to be the friend and scribbles what he thinks of this **BORING CLASS**.

Chinmay Kar

BORING CLASS

A boring class! What to do?
Ideally sitting is such a pain, listening to it too

Body is in class but mind is not
That's why, writing these is the idea I got

People write anything when they get bored
That's when these ideas emerge where it's stored

Some imagine dreams while some play games
That's when people like me think, coming to class was bane

We don't have courage in class to play
Neither the mind agrees to stay

Having a burning sensation, we however sit
What teacher's teaching, nothing goes in a bit

So here I am writing all these
And later copying this masterpiece

Will show it to those interested
Shall we stop before getting busted?

Well turns out am still not busted
And don't know how to continue what we have started

Still the boring class continues
But I see some are having different views

First benchers are writing a lot
Irony is, I have no idea of what we are getting taught

Heart speaks to mind that you can read at home
Will finish it, whether there is quake, tsunami or storm

But the thing about heart is, we can't trust it
God knows what question in exams, we will be getting
hit

So now my mind is also not having words to get it
finished
Slowly the advice of heart is getting diminished
At last! Am waiting for the class to get over
Imagining the comfort of getting a decent shower

The classes still continued one after the other with no trace of coming to an end. Idly sitting in a chair meant punishing his sportive mind and body. Even writing his thoughts was getting him bored as he had already used up all his brain's power to think of words.

Restlessness growing in him was making him mad, and he was desperately trying to divert his mind by counting how many times the teacher says a peculiar word or does a mistake or slacks off. It's strange how we try to find the fault of others when we get bored. It's the same as the saying goes "Idle mind is devil's workshop". Charan like anybody else lost the hope of ever getting his mind to stay in the boundaries of class room and eventually drifted afar to **TRAVEL BEING STATIC.**

TRAVELLING STATIC

Who says our mind is stable and fixed
It can roam whenever it gets jinxed

All it needs is a soft and slow rhythm
And then a new poem in mind gets redeemed

Yes I travelled the world in minutes
Sitting stable but running loose with no limits

Yes I felt the freshness of mountains
Drank the water poured from heaven

Yes I ran through the deserts
Under sun, wearing sweaty shirt

Yes I sat on the chairs in the beach
Listened carefully to those birds preach

Yes I surfed on the ocean wave
Oh my! Many gadgets from water to save

Yes I swam being free and sassy

Yes I flew being happy and breezy

All of these in matter of seconds

Sitting in my class before making amends

At last … Do you feel the same?

Or am I the only one? Please don't blame

He was about to drown in his deeper thoughts when he heard the noise of a door slammed in front of them, as the teacher stormed off complaining about the present generation and how ill brought up are they. Apparently she took this big step when she realised that clearing the boredom of the students are beyond her control and that she could no longer tolerate their behaviour in the class room and teach effectively. She warned and gave one last chance and had tried everything to ignore but still students didn't even reply to her when she asked do we follow her.

Though her storm off didn't change the environment there but it had quite an effect on Charan. The bitter words of her mentor got him thinking if it is really true what she said. Was there some problem with his generation? He looked around to see everyone gazing on the flashy 6-inch screens which they call "smart" but is making them dumb.

Was it really the **OLD MIND** which has become tired or is it the **YOUNG THOUGHTS** which has gone corrupted?

———— ◆ ————

Chinmay Kar

OLD MIND YOUNG THOUGHTS

It's hard to remember those cherishing days
Then, whatever the situation we would find a way

Is it the mind which has grown old or is it maturity
Everything in world seems complex with ambiguity

There was a time we used to find happiness in nature
Now everyone's busy racing on how to become faster

Don't know, maybe nowadays motto is "Be sharper, find answer"
But no one ever asks, are you ok my teacher?

There was a time when we were lost
But they would guide us with endless trust

They would share us the universes secrets
And would take us through the journey with free tickets

But again, don't know whether mind has grown old or is
it maturity

Being selfish, we never ask about their difficulties

Is it the time which has rusted the mind to take them for
granted?

Maybe it's the map of them which has all the secrets
charted

Now we don't have the courage to stand up against
injustice … affecting our behaviour

There is always honour for legends and heroes but never
for saviour

If growing old makes us this, then why not grow young?

If it's the fault of maturity, then why not replace it with
simplicity?

It was early noon and after taking a shower in the common room, he marches to his most favourite place of the hospital, "The Surgical wards" where all the patients before or after having a surgery get admitted. Being there was his favourite way of killing time as everyone would have a different story to narrate and who doesn't like to know everything about someone else.

Sharing smiles with a complete stranger and collecting tears of others, all can be seen in that same room. He always would let the relatives speak all the information, be it of his importance or not. But he always targets himself to never let someone pity on themselves. With this in his mind, he found himself in front of a sick 10-year-old kid who was admitted due to a genetic condition of blood disorder.

Due to his disease, that boy never had the chance of living like a perfectly healthy kid ever. His condition demands of being wrapped up in chains with his bed and never do anything as invasive as opening a bottle with a can opener because his body would be in a constant pain 24*7.

But it got Charan astonished as he saw the kid being perfectly fine and was far away from pitying his life or curse his condition. He was laughing, giggling and playing around with the nurses coming to measure his temperature and pulse. He also didn't feel shame to sing, dance and play with his toys.

When asked about the secret of his inspiration, the child replied in an instant to Charan that it was not long ago that he was pitying on himself but got the answer of his **BLEEDING DESIRE**.

BLEEDING DESIRE

Storm's coming so I closed my eyes
Feeding heart with the same old lies

Outside world's so boring
That's why everyone stays in buildings

Rain outside is the same water falling from shower
Boys I see playing outside are cowards

Those were things I heard from mom years ago
Believed it true, now realised it's all pseudo

Oh God! Why can't I go once and …
See the stormy sky
Play games that are not rubber toys

Run on mud and feel like flying
Appreciate the rainbow when sun is shining

Slowly felt my own breath and thought am good for
nothing

That's when saw a light saying I had to intervene

Don't lose faith child! You are precious
Light said, "Pay attention, this is serious"

I have sent everyone with equal sorrow and happiness
So what if you feel pale and dizziness

It's not like your condition snatches your jubilance
It's your attitude towards it which needs vigilance

Don't let your doubts pull you from what you want
Don't always say to yourself that you can't

For all we know, Heaven and Hell both lay here
Depends on what you want to see, feel and hear

Those who don't have any weakness get medal for
bravery
But those who turn their weakness into strength are truly
legendary.

"Turning weakness into strength", that last line in which the boy ended his narration to Charan got him thinking as to how he can implement the same in his life. Was it his simplicity which is dragging him from his success?

He never misses a chance and begs everyone to point out his mistakes so that he can judge himself and rectify it but no one ever does that. Ultimately he has now encountered a stage of self-realisation where he thinks that everyone thinks him to be naïve and simple. It was this nature of him which has dragged him from his victory.

He would think so much of dragging everyone with him to success that he would always lose that window of opportunity where if he would have become a bit selfish then he would be in a better place in life now.

He pondered over these thoughts when the headline of the news channel stole his attention. It was in big letters saying "Terror on the Rock shore valley has stunned the people living there and has forced everyone to stay inside as multiple attacks in The Trinity Mall have been reported throughout".

Charan got stunned as the breaking news flashed and changed its colours from Black to Red and Black again saying 18 cops were shot dead by the terrorists. Everyone stopped doing their chores as it was the silence before a major storm would be hitting the ceilings and floors of this hospital.

It was only that time when he realised that he should have drunk water when he was feeling thirsty. He swallowed all the saliva which he could gather at that time and gulped it like a pirate drinking rum before pulling off a heist as he looked the CCTV footage of the demons **MASKED UNDERNEATH**.

MASKED UNDERNEATH

Random attacks in city

Pay attention, it's not a story

Wasn't it enough to attack Taj, Nariman and Oberoi

Terrorist's painted the day with colour red

Eighteen mothers came to know about their sons' death

Why this cruelty? Why give pain?

This home nurtured hatred will give you no gain

What was the fault of those martyrs?

All that's left are their blood soaked gears

Are some square inch of land worth lives?

Does no one know, if we unite, everyone will thrive

We are the same standing in different religious queues

Things differing are our cast, creed and personal views

Why not just stop this bloodshed
And lift the darkness in people pasted

Distribute flowers which blossom
Instead of guns which are fearsome

Why not spread love together
Instead of taking lives of each other

Everything is fair in love and war
But living a happy life has its own charm.

It was a nightmare inside the white walls. All the nurse stations were hyperactive as everyone got briefed about the situation. Some were preparing all the gurneys while some were busy stashing all the frozen blood waiting to be transfused. Some were calling their homes, warning their loved ones to stay indoors. Meanwhile hospital opened up its emergency gates as the ambulances rushed inside each carrying a victim in critical situation.

Some were multiple shot injuries, whereas some were severe head trauma. All the doctors were called off from their break as it was a "All hands on deck" situation. Charan successfully resuscitated two crashing victims while securing airway for another. He filled up his mind with all his favourite songs he could think of so that he doesn't get nervous.

In his entire career till now, he had never dreamt of being a part of something big. His mind was half drowned with enthusiasm whereas the other half was swimming in the waves of fear.

He thanked God of making him a part of all this and prayed that no critical victim dies of any negligence. There were some cases where he felt what should he do? Should he stop? He knows nothing can be done theoretically but practically can't he do better. He pressed all his weights as he cracks open a victims chest to surgically correct a cardiac emboli and telling himself constantly that the **BROKEN CAN BE MENDED**.

BROKEN CAN BE MENDED

Ever felt the deep endless pain which you can't see

Binding you with the chains of regret, not letting you freeze

Asking yourself where to go?

To the right where emptiness is left

Or to the left where nothing seems right

In my view …

Way of living has two options

What you choose depends on your actions

Either let the circumstance change you

Or wake up every day saying my life is new

Embracing the fact that ups and downs go side by side

So you have to balance it by right time to seek and hide

Chinmay Kar

If you have talent, then make the opportunity

If you don't then wait for opportunity

But no guarantee that opportunities will make you
satisfied

Because fact is we are never satisfied

When our present seems bad, we blame the past

When present seems good, we fear for future

We should always remember

What's broken can be mended

Suffering can get faded

You have to ask, along the process, what have you learnt

That moral … inscribe it bright like it's freshly burnt

Let everyone feel your deep stored passion

Set yourself as the example for future generations

Along the way, find your redemption, don't forsake

Remember, the day you find, that would be your last
mistake.

The clock was ready to strike 4:00 as the victims were slowly getting settled, and the surge of patients had passed its peak. After so much of active strain, Charan at last got his grab on a glass full of water. He was just going to drink all of it in a sip when he heard someone crying. He looked around to discover a man with a freshly amputated left hand.

The poor man had just only regained his consciousness to find a bandage in his elbow instead of a full forearm with which he was sipping coffee a few hours back just before he got thrown two storeys out from the window by the crowd getting scared of hearing gun shots. Charan immediately turned towards the man asking whether he could be of any service to him.

The man had clearly known that it was the doctors who had cut his hands and showed a mixed expression of anger and sorrow to Charan. Charan too quickly sensed the emotions of the man and offered his glass of water.

Through a quick nod with his head, the man spilled the water offered by Charan. "You wretched devils! How dare you cut my hand? Who gave you the authority? Do you know what you have done? I was simply enjoying the day so that I can finally do my dream job! I had longed and hoped to work in this company and was in the brink. What will I do now? My life has ended and it's all because of you …. You heartless butchers!"

Charan waited for the guy to cool down and explained him the situation that they had to cut his arm; otherwise, he would have died of infection.

"Saved from dying you say?" The poor guy laughed hopelessly, "What good is this life than dying now?".

"See mister, whatever be the situation in life, be it all your limbs cut off from you … never, I say, never think life to be that cheap!". How can you think of dying when the mind which compels you to die is still living?

You say that your dream job has gone away, no worries, it's not like you were born to serve in that job or that the company was made so that you could join there. Things change, companies change even people change. Why can't your dreams change?

You would be thinking to ask me one good example on how your life can be better? I have many examples to tell you and it's all derived from things you can't imagine. These are the **TINY INSPIRATIONS** which forces you to go fearless.

<u>TINY INSPIRATION</u>

Once in blue moon, ever observed wind chime closely
Cheering us with her song even hanging lonely

Summer, winter, autumn or spring; we love the tune
heartily
Even when sad or happy, chime never forgets its duty

So, why not become like chime and sing everyone a
happy song
Because, true happiness is when heart and mind work
along

Again, ever marked a door hinge closely

Trying best to close the door when wind gushes rapidly

That little thing's responsible for giving us relaxed sleep

If door hinges can be that uptight, why can't we care that
deep?

Again, ever seen a door lock closely

We leave possessions behind, trusting it fully

Chinmay Kar

Having a door lock, don't you feel safe?

Protection's done by lock, still we act brave

So the big picture is:

You can derive inspiration from every little thing

Be inspired, Do your work, don't look back and see what
success brings

With that moving speech, Charan was sure that he would die of thirst if he doesn't get hold himself of some water. The poor man was also moved listening to that speech but again started looking at his cut elbow and succumbed to his pain. Charan gave a mild sedative to the man so that he feels drowsy and takes rest.

He quickly again rushed to the emergency ward after he had his mouthful of water. He stretched his hands and relieved pressure on his neck as he started measuring the pulse and blood pressure of all the stabilised patients with his stethoscope which he was wearing in the morning. Who knew that his flashy branded newly bought stethoscope which still smells new would come handy this early?

Though mild the ambulances still kept coming with every patient being in a less priority list. His fellow mate had gone tired after giving everyone first aid. His friend Aaron was just going to collapse in the ground as Charan got hold of him in a semi-reclined manner.

He quickly poured some glucose in his friend's mouth and offered him water. Though being a former basketball player, Aaron regretted himself of getting fatigued. Having lost all hope, in a semi-conscious state, he uttered the words, "We would need a miracle to handle this situation. God! What will happen?"

After a while everyone got busy in their own work, handling the patients assigned to them. Charan on his inside was loaded with questions and uncertainty. That question kept coming in his mind ..., "Will any miracle happen?", "Why is it taking time to happen?". Does really something like **MIRACLE** exist?

MIRACLES

Miracles do happen … if you want it,
Changing your perception … if you let it

Like success means hard work getting opportunity
Miracles happen when hopes become reality,

Just have to take the path with no pressure,
And witness a thousand miracles to capture

But even miracles take a little time
You need to make devotion and intelligence rhyme

Have a little faith and believe in your hard work
Don't hesitate when you get that stroke of luck

So never stop believing in hopes
Gamble everything to cross that slope

Because stars are ready to shower
It's you who has to show the power

Feel that rush flowing through the veins
Boosting and churning every place of that brain

Brace! There will be spectators to watch
Ascend! And lead everyone along the path.

Decide … if you want to show your fall or rise
Whether sensing that dedication, even God also cries.

Show the fate that impossible is still possible,
It needs only that spirit wearing coats of miracles.

The daylight was slowly disappearing and the clock was ready to strike 6. The incoming of patients was finally over and Charan had just gone to update himself with the news to know the whereabouts of the attackers. Did they get caught? What was their purpose? Will they get strict punishment? He had just finished getting his eyes fixed on the small letters below travelling in light speed in the news update bar when his ears heard the siren noise of multiple police vehicles parking outside the emergency gates in a fashioned way.

The sheriff of the Rock shore valley, a man in his 50s with a round, bulged abdomen and a dead serious look in his face. He itched his long thick moustache as he entered the premises with his team. "Emergency rescue squad" is what he called his team as he showed off his silver badge with 4 stars and summoned the chief doctor in charge.

The senior doctor enquired about the situation and the purpose of their visit. The sheriff in a serious look asked the doctor to gather a team of trustworthy doctors and meet him inside a room where he can talk privately. Don't know what it was but the terrorised look in the face of sheriff depicted that something very serious and bad is going to happen if they don't get hold of the situation and make it right.

As a dedicated doctor and a man responsible to his duties, Charan was the first person chosen as the member of trusted doctors, and they suddenly went into a closed room used to store the extra hospital stuffs. The sheriff with the same terrorised looks stated, "Fellow doctors, I deeply regret to inform you that among the injured patients which you received, there is one who actually is himself an attacker and had injured himself purposefully to gain access to your hospital and strike terror among the hearts of the people. Their motive is to convey that, even in the safest place where everyone gets the chance to heal, they can still strike terror. No place is safe!".

All the handful doctors who were just starting to breathe in comfort trembled as they got to know that they were living under the same roof with an attacker and that one of them would have actually offered is treatment to him only so that he can rightfully strike again.

The sheriff reassured saying that everything is going to be alright as his task force has arrived. All he asks is to keep this information with themselves and help the task force under covered acting like sick people and guide them throughout the hospital. "Be an extra set of eyes ... Activate Code black" is what he said to complete his briefing.

Charan came out of the room with a determined look to offer everything he could while Aaron trembled as he walked alongside him. "How can you be that stabled? Don't you fear that every breath which you are taking might be your last? How can you be that fearless? God knows ... what will be our fate?" Fate? You ask what our fate is. See mate ... look at those innocent faces who are smiling .... A few hours ago they were coming in crying their heart out, who would have thought that they would forget about what had happened to them this fast? Can you see their happy and satisfied look now? It's the hope which has kept them alive and its hope which is keeping me alive and running. For all I know is that my views on **STORY OF FATE** can be told on some other day.

Chinmay Kar

THE STORY OF FATE

Prepare yourself, cause this is a story of fate,

Am sure no one understands it, I bet

Is it a predetermined script that you will pass that gate?

Well, let me tell you …

If life is a paper, it is its font,

It's everything you wanted, everything you don't

At some point it's sure you and fate will confront

Don't know if it will change you

But it sure will shape your career's queue

This is your companion that controls your destiny,

Embrace it and it will till end, accompany

Deny it, and it will be the reason of your mockery

Some prayers get answered and some prayers don't

Will that make you disheartened? It won't

Lost that perfect good opportunity? Don't cry,

Next time don't hesitate to try

Start trying again when you lost that belief

Feel that rush in your hands, fate will make you achieve.

Some doors will swing open while some doors will close

Remember, going down that novel path means opening
page of new prose

You will see what you want to see when you are ready,

All it takes is your decision when to run, when be steady

You have to become perfect for that perfect chance

Till that hold on and let go things to make balance

Remember

Fate doesn't control you, it's you who controls fate,

All it needs is

A pinch of belief, a spoon of courage and drops of hard
work,

Sip it and see how it tastes.

Wandering all over the hospital, Charan regrets on his choice of wearing his noisy boots today as he sneaks around the other wards to find any nuisance which can grab attention. He was just about to take the second right from the corridor when he marked a shadow in the distant left. A shadow of a man desperately trying to find something, and a cold chill throughout the spine was felt by Charan as he silently signals Aaron to follow him.

Chasing the shadow led them to a newly constructed hospital wing. Although its construction was near to over as it lacked its final functional approval, the management was planning to open it soon for the public to improve its hospitality.

Recalling the events of construction made Charan remember that the engineers were planning to replace all the circuit wirings and were attempting to move the main switch to the newly established block.

If the attacker wants to strike terror in hospital, his motive would be to switch off the main lines so that all the patients would die of lack of oxygen. A very violent form of death … to choke in a place which is meant to restore life. It was a speciality of Charan to use his mind web of overthinking to make an intelligent guess. Although not every time but in situation like this has helped him more than he could think of.

Even thinking it in mind was such horrific that Charan lost his balance and was about to fall down one storey down but his position was quickly replaced by his 'mate' who fell down in a brutal manner to injure himself. "Aaaaaagh! Oh God! Why is it happening to me? What did I do to get this type of torture, oh God!" Aaron cried out loud narrating all which had happened to him that day.

From falling unconscious to hearing patients scold him about their bad luck .... He had heard it all and was on the verge to lose his calm when he fell in a horrific painful way.

Charan asked him to get up for which he replied, "Why? Only to fall again? Only to die properly in the hand of that attacker? Or to die by the hands of those whom I try to save? Why?".

Charan says, "You ask me why? See mate, it's not like that you only in the whole world is suffering now .... There may be someone else who is suffering more than you but still would be holding on to hope. Then why can't you! Now I would like to ask you **WHY?**".

WHY

Why do we smile? Even on bad days
When actually, we should cry for faults of yesterday

Why do we dream? Even when not asleep
When we actually, should doze in deep

Why do we try? Even when we know we'll lose
When we actually, should have never chose

Why do we giggle? Even at bad times
When there should be tears in eyes

Why do we climb? Even being on top
When actually, it's time to stop

Why do we work? Even on Sundays
When we actually, should enjoy holidays

Why do we run? Even when legs are tired
When we should stick to the bed being wired

The answer to all this, my friend is HOPE

Charan finds a way to reach to Aaron and delivers him a first aid with what he could find nearby. Aaron was silent after what Charan had spoken to him and followed him like a faithful companion. They quickly sneaked around the place where the main switch was set up. It was in a distant that the switch was spotted by Aaron while Charan spotted the attacker aware of them being here and aware of the whereabouts of the main switch by the loud noise of Aaron.

It was a race against time; Charan had quickly calculated that it would take him 10 minutes to reach the main switch while the attacker can reach there in 5 minutes. Charan forgot about any other safe measures and jumped and ran through its way to reach the main switch. The attacker had a grin in his face as he knew that he can reach there first. Charan thrusted all his force in his legs … forgot all the jogging which he did just 12 hours ago … forgot about all the running which he did about 2 hours ago in the wards … forgot that his cells don't have any source of energy as he had foolishly skipped his meals.

It was in this time when his sportive built actually helped him as he jumped from one floor to the other like a monkey rushing to grab his food. Aaron stood on the opposite end as he watched Charan and the attacker rushing for the main switch. He prayed to all the Gods which had ever existed or will exist or just exist throughout the time to help Charan go fast. May not the evil mind win in God's presence? Once he switches off the main lines, they can't bring switch on the power as the wiring across that whole area was jumbled. He started throwing anything which he could break and threw him towards that devil seeking human souls as he came close enough within his firing range.

The race was about to end as the attacker despite of all the things thrown at him was going to pull off the switch when BaaaaaaaaM! A hard wooden lodge fell right over his head and he fell down being disoriented. "BULL'S EYE!" Aaron shouted as he recognised that his shooting is still perfect, thinking about his old high school memories filled with basketball matches and finally taking a deep satisfied breath.

It was just a matter of seconds when Charan reached there and grabbed the man by his collar. As well versed with anatomy, he locked all his joints by tricky movement and dragged him towards the hospital.

There was no sense of happiness or relief in the face of Charan. Everyone clapped for his heroism and sheriff himself shook his head but all he did was returned the gesture. He also realised that it was 7 making his shift for the day to end. He bid bye to all the doctors and dragged himself to the common dressing room.

He changed to a fresh pair of clothes and thought about all his experiences. He had always thought that everything in life is destined and everything holds a purpose. Was this day trying to tell him something? When is this day going to end? Does this day want something from me? Do I have to **DECIDE** something?

———◈———

DECIDE

So tell me ... Have you ever experienced the pain of
being alone
Owning latest gadgets but knowing no one will call the
phone

Listening to music where the singers sing along

Telling yourself "That's where you should belong"

Laughing like they do .... Enjoying like they do

Living life to its fullest, showing everyone the potential
you grew

But these are all fragments which one day dreams

Like eating a salty snack expecting taste of cream

This is the bitter sharp pointy truth of life

Being good doesn't guarantee not getting stabbed with
knife

Nothing goes according to the plan you want

But there isn't a situation to solve you can't

If it's the way of riding life to hop on

I would pat myself and say bring it on

Enough has been told enough to actually say it's
ENOUGH

This is a drastic change in me and it's really tough

If being simple and truthful leads to face disregard

Then it's about time to show them the wild card

I would graciously accept the pain in my heart

Truth be told, fear of pain ignites the body to start

As the peculiar long day came to an end, Charan starts his engine and drives off to the roads. He is not planning to go home.

All he wants is to spend some quality time with himself as after watching so much sadness of all the people throughout the day and providing them your own share of happiness takes a toll on you. Only the one who provides to everyone usually gets deprived of the same.

He was in a state where all the loneliness in his mind would come surging in if he had not left that place where he showed his heroism. In this state of watching too much co-incidences, he was desperately trying to **DISCOVER DELIGHT.**

<u>DISCOVERING DELIGHT</u>

Oh simple thing! Where have you gone
I am getting impatient and don't know where have come

I came across an empty barn to feel earth in my feet
So tell me life, why has the circumstance gone this steep

Oh simple thing! Where have you gone
I feel losing track of time and mind turning to stone

I came across a fallen tree and grieved its memories
Was this the tree which held still while I relished
sceneries

Oh simple thing! Where have you gone
I feel getting old and needs something to rely on

I walked across a dry river which had once refreshing
nectar
Is that the place where I wanted to rest but always
switched for later

So, let's allow the thoughts breaking in
All the bad memories sabotaging

And let our heart hold fast
For this shall soon pass

Like the high tide dragging the sand

All your fears will end as the sun rises again
You will never know when it happened, when it began

Life has its own rules and this is the way it ends
Nothing is meaningless, so live life with no regrets

Why not live life to its fullest
Avoid the stress by being the coolest

When there is doubt, always remember there is someone
above
Preparing to welcome you to his humble abode

For the iron which gets more beaten

Is the one which leaves the dark dungeon

Finding a little peace, he decided to drive himself to the sea shore to loosen up. All he wanted was a little peace which he got deprived of throughout the day. His phone was exploding with messages from Priya about how the day was? Is there anything wrong in mountain valley? Oh God! Is this right? Has really a terror attack happened? Whatever, just be alright and stay away from trouble? Hey, why are you not texting me? Have you forgotten me? At least leave a message! It's called courtesy? I get it you remain very busy and all, but are you the president? Don't you have even 2 seconds to spare and text that it's all right? Uggh! Whatever ….

Charan sighed as he scrolled down the texts. He was just fed up of always being the saviour for everyone while no one really cares to return the same to him. With the thought that at least his mother would spend time with him … he drove off to the seashore to feel the **BREEZY VIBES**.

BREEZY VIBES

So there I was enjoying
Feeling the breeze in the sea beach

Deep in thoughts, am swimming
It was a needed break to get wounded mind stitched

Saw the gradual rising of waves while I sat
Cut off the internet, switched off all chat

Didn't want to leave even if I get wet
Well that's the purest form of peace I bet

Sometimes you have to put aside your tension
Just leave them behind the platform of station

And hop on this amazing and peaceful train
I guarantee you no pain but much to gain

Take this journey to connect with your inner self
Straighten the things which got tangled themselves

Be the light of your faded shadow
Water still wets even if it's shallow

Be the dark of your shining ego
Sour the taste even if it's a mango

There will be problems in life no doubt
Will you let them in? Or knock them out?

There are ups and downs in life; be careful
But keep the spirit, view at end is beautiful

Fear of falling down makes you climb up
So, be a force of nature, no one can stop

Balance life with equal happiness and sadness

If you get too happy ... Don't become reckless
If you get too sad ... Don't become depressed

While getting refreshed by the breezy waves of the sea, he couldn't resist but notice some children playing football along the coast.

They had no sign of worry or tension or regret. The smile which they were imparting was the purer form which Charan also had when he was a kid. Childhood memories kept entering his mind and how the complexity of the world has changed his view on life. How he would play till his legs burnt out from and mom would call to wash hands and order to start doing homework of school.

Tears dropped from the same eyes which had a responsible look this morning as he remembered simplicity of the childhood and how he would bet everything only to spend some time reliving the past. How it all changed in just a blink!

SOMEWHERE IN BETWEEN, everything had changed.

Chinmay Kar

SOMEWHERE BETWEEN

Picture it's 2003, you are watching "Shaka Laka Boom Boom" on Starplus or "Shararat" or "Kyunki Saas Bhi Kabhi Bahu Thi" with your mother. Drinking Rasna, Horlicks. "Kal Ho Na Ho" is your favourite song!

School is tomorrow

Can someone remember those good old days, those simpler times?

Those are now turned to dust, kept in memories and packed in a pretty good looking album

Someone in the journey between 2003 and 2018 …. A lot had happened

One's chasing for sweets, now are chasing for money

That time, we were crude and simple, now we are refined and changed and everything is just complicated

Somewhere between chasing pets to chasing Pokemon; we changed

Somewhere between grocery shop to Flipkart and Amazon; we changed

Somewhere between piggy bank to Paytm; we changed

Somewhere between watching Mahabharat to watching
Game of Thrones; we changed

Somewhere between Raja, Rani, Chor, Police to Mini
Militia and Bullet Force; we changed

Somewhere between shaking hands to tapping a wave in
FaceBook; we changed

Somewhere between smelling new books to
downloading e-books; we changed

Somewhere between picking our mother from baazar to
picking up girlfriend from mall; we changed

Somewhere between washing powder Nirma to Closer
and Despacito; we changed

And so the list goes on ....

Chinmay Kar

Having all these transitions on our life, facing all these
changes

Are we adapting? Are we the change?

Are we the last few remnants of the past?

Or

Are we the stepping stone of future.

It was not too long when he had relived acquiring all the memories of then when his phone again buzzed with a simple message "I think it's as long as we can go .... This is the end of line ... I can't continue to live like this, I don't know what our relationship means but I think we should end it here before it advances any further ... so good bye, Charan".

Before reading the message till the end, Charan had already started his car and flew his car to Priya's house. All he wanted was some rest, his intention was never to hurt Priya. He thought all of the things which he would tell to Priya as he parked his car in front of Priya's lawn and rang the bell. In his mind, Charan had already portrayed a picture of Priya who would be busy worrying about him throughout the day.

Maybe her eyes would be red due to all the crying which she would have been done throughout the day. How bad of me ... maybe she was right; I would have at least texted her but what could I have done ... my phone was in the common room and I never got the chance or had a break to go and collect phone and text her ... yes maybe she will understand. With all these thoughts in mind, Charan's jaws dropped when he saw Priya.

She was having glowy eyes instead of eyes he had imagined, showing herself to be in a festive vibe. There was no trace of any regret or worry in Priya's voice when she uttered the same words as her text messages right in front of the face of a man who was appreciated for his bravery and slammed the door right in front of him telling to go and never come back. Charan still tried to explain everything to her from outside but soon realised that Priya was not listening to him and had gone somewhere inside.

It was only after Charan had scolded himself of how careless he can be when he heard some distant noises coming from the backyard. When he reached there to investigate, he got shocked watching Priya sneaking from the backdoor and hopping in her friend's car screaming "Party's on ...". It took no time for Charan to understand that the reason behind the party was to celebrate their survival from the attack. Charan broke into pieces when he marked that Priya was actually happy and showed no sign of regret for her loss of friendship with him.

The atmosphere suddenly changed and a thunder was heard in the distant sky as the party car drove off to the mountains. Charan was still locked in the same position for about 10 minutes. He didn't even try to call Priya when he had the chance or go back to his car. Slowly a slash of wind accompanied by heavy rain poured all over the mountain valley. Not clear what made Charan to move but he slowly moved towards his car ... with his face filled with **FLASH TEARS**.

<u>FLASH TEARS</u>

So there was this gusty wind and a heavy rain, still I
didn't care about drenching and walked down the street
for my car. At that time, I was thinking …

Call me a boy, am just being a simple man

Where should I go, I have got no plan

One more time, it's all slipping like sand

Everyone sees it, no one cares to lend a hand

With this thought, I started my car and may have done a
little rash driving. A part of me was saying …

See my friend this is the way life goes,

Pain is sharper, deeper the memories are stored

All the memories, imagined with these eyes

Saw it all drifting away in the skies.

And with that dilemma in my mind, I saw an old couple
taking the footpath and sharing an umbrella. Both were
moving away from the umbrella so that the other one
doesn't get wet, resulting in both getting drenched. Then
I thought …

Chinmay Kar

I want to be that man holding that umbrella

Want that affection that can't be found in a car or a villa

Being a slight jealous of that old man, I drove my car to
the place I call my redemption palace. The rain had
stopped so I parked my car, stretched my legs and …

Looked at the stars at night

Looked at the sky while they turned off the lights

I said …

Hello there, the angel of my nightmare

Got no one for me but you who cares

Maybe you will be the one that saves me

Remember, this is an old rusted and broken heart, please
bear me.

Tears have come down and mixed with rain

Imagine the memories we'd make, I'll not let that go in
vain

These drops of sadness are still falling down

But I hope you'll say, "I'll not let you drown".

I mean it what I say, when I say, until my dying day

So don't let go for a moment ever, please stay.

Our mutual trust would be the one no one could break

I know you ... you know me, and that thing no one can take.

I hope you see that deep pain I hide in my smile

And wash that pain like stain, like I do with my style.

Many have asked, what is your type? My answer ...

I have got one foot in fire, and other in a river

Waiting for the one who drags my foot to flowers.

With a confused look, he stared at the sky full of stars. He just wanted to find the answer of what holds value in this life?

Why if life so damn confusing? The events occurred throughout the day had made him contradict himself with his past self. What should I do? Where shall I go? Well as always it's me being alone! He vaguely remembered how he woke up today. The way of life which he remembered today now has become a laughing stock to him. He repeatedly slapped himself hard uttering how naïve he is.

Still trying to find what is wrong and what is right … why is there not a crash course teaching us how to live life? It would have been better if someone would be present every time to guide us through the difficult phases of life in this complex world, to guide us where to go … **TO THE LEFT? WAIT … RIGHT.**

LEFT...WAIT RIGHT?

Where should I go ...? To the

Left? Where society challenges me
Right? Where I challenge the society

Left? Where the mind pulls the string
Right? Where the heart points my dreams

Left? Where I make the challenges
Right? Where the challenges make me

Left? Where I will pull myself extreme
Right? Where I will crawl to be supreme

Left? Where I will live those old dreams
Right? Where I will make my new dreams

Left? Where there may be still hope
Right? Where there is new scope

Left? Where there is unfinished business
Right? Where there is new access

Chinmay Kar

Left? Where there are uncharted waters
Right? Where you know every centimetre

Between this Left and Right is how we grow
Funny thing is, whatever you do, it's never going to go

Because as always … we think that

right is always Right

AND

left should be Left

It's strange how we...the human beings have itself complicated this life...this life would never have got complicated if everyone would have just simply share their feelings directly. Say directly how much they know and judge people straight in front of their faces. Maybe this complexity in this world grew because so many people for so many generations have not been true to themselves. It's this nature of being silent when one should speak but they won't.

They always remain silent....No doubt they want to help, want to be friends, want to share everything, want to tell everything, only 'want' never do. It's this juggling of their feelings which sometimes becomes **IN AND OUT.**

Chinmay Kar

IN AND OUT

It's shivering cold outside,
While it's waging war inside

It's funny how you pretend to smile outside

When really you are collecting tears inside

It's bravery when you try acting stupid outside

Don't want to let anyone know what the situation is
inside

It's smart when you play rock music outside

Meanwhile, slow music comforts slowly inside

It's strange how the day passes by outside

And you are stuck in an endless moment inside

It's cunning to let everyone know your secrets outside

Keeping that precious one deep inside

It's sad how everyone acts tough outside

But treat the bleeding part silently inside

It's shame when someone acts like a new leaf outside

Actually masking the dead leaf with fragile colours
inside

But the toughest times are …

When the inside emerges out to show itself outside

And the thought strikes "Oops! No place to hide".

Hide! Hiding is the only thing which we the humans have excelled in doing. It has been done so much that it has now got incorporated in our genes and is getting passed on to the next generations. One doesn't need to learn this; we have inherited it which gets unlocked during this prime age. With all these hidings and finally knowing in the hard way that happiness come to only those who seek it himself, Charan finally decides to let go off all the burdens.

Burdens of helping others, struggling throughout night only so that no one other than him has to face problems, desperately trying to sell one's own heart in the market full of cheaters, devils and liars....He has finally learned that to be in peace, one just simply has to shut his doors in his mind.

Finally coming into this conclusion, he remembers all his feelings for Priya for one last time and finally **LETS GO**.

<u>LETTING GO</u>

What can I say? Am a simple poet doing my Poetry?
And I guess you specialise trapping folks with flattery

Not proud to say, I am also a victim of that
But I hope that today or tomorrow you face God's wrath

Because what you did was not just only wrong
Enough to stop my beats…it was that strong

Though it was for mere seconds, it felt like an era
Felt all those memories deleted like a flash of camera

But you know what, everything happens for a reason,
maybe it was meant to be

Maybe you think that you weren't loved widely but you
were loved deeply

You just thought me to be random person in your life

Who was funny, simple, useful at time but was never
your type

Chinmay Kar

Now I will not say that you coming in life, taught a
lesson

Because you know what, maybe you were important to
me once but now an old fashion

Can't have you sitting next to me driving my car

Just want to say, you failed…My ride has gone too far

There are some things in life you can't have because you
don't deserve

Maybe your prize awaits you for that right moment well
preserved

After thinking and clearing out his mind, he finally reaches his flat sharp at 9, changes his clothes to night dress and prepares to give rest to all the body which felt relaxed for the first time in his life. He stretches his legs in his bed while the cotton pillows clear away his neck ache.

For the first time, he didn't plan out as to what he should do the next day and embraced the fact that every day should come as new to him with new difficulties and new rewards. He prepares to go to a deep sleep while reconciling with his past in this **FOREVER NIGHT**.

FOREVER NIGHT

Who are you? What are you? Why have you come?
Standing outside my window like a peeping tom

Weaving the coats of fear, comes in the middle of night
Laughing at myself when the dark is the most bright

Watching you from the corner of my bed, I fright
Still am compelled to observe fearing I may lose sight

Sometimes I think oh poor soul what have you become
Without any roof, you roam around even in storm

Either searching from happiness or terrorising people
Sucking out our belief from God and temples

I know thinking about you gives you even more power
But it's about time to search and seek your answer

Even living grows tired then why not also dead?
Why not learn to forget knowing this is the way it ends

Catharsis

I address your good self
You are fed up of haunting and I with fearing

So give a break to yourself
And just like that the clock is ticking and ticking

As the clock ticked and ticked, that young boy who woke up that day with mind full of doubts finally had found the answers. Now he is sleeping in his bed ... holding his pillows like a baby who grabs the hand of his mother and sleeps in the bed making a semi-circle. And just like that the young boy, after making amends with his haunted past self, drifted to his last experience of **DEADLOCK DILEMMA**.

THE DEADLOCK DILEMMA

In the oceans deep, there lies an innocent boy
Doesn't know why he is there and why there is no joy.

For all he knows is that he was once a jolly good lad
Faced with cheat and deception wants to become bad.

Till now he had thought to walk along
Now wants to leave everything and be alone.

As always said, no one really understands what you feel
Sometimes you have to isolate and take a kneel.

Now the mind tells the boy to don't cry
To get out, just let your attachments die.

The arrow has stabbed your heart and now it's broken
Don't look back this is the path you have chosen.

You have to crawl yourself out from the memories
There is no temporary escape from these miseries.

The decision is like a bitter sweet between his teeth
Though in water, he feels sweaty because of heat.

He feels shaky and hears a whisper
Counts up his mistakes as he shivers.

The broken heart says stick with me oh my best friend
Things we fought for don't deserve this end.

Don't leave me, all the time you were always there
Lost in depth of darkness, see the light shining there.

Because that is the dream we both hoped for
Remember, remember all we fight for.

Come on, put your hands in your chest
Don't be afraid to face life's challenging tests.

At last the boy got himself pulled from the oceans deep
Woke up in his bed with an unforgettable sleep.

———◆———

EPILOGUE

JOURNEY THROUGH DECADES

It is a story of a boy

His journey of becoming a man

It's not much time when he used to play toys

Now with goggles, beard and a bit of skin tan

There was once when he would catch bus to go to school

Pack lunch in a stuffed tiffin and share it in the recess

Time passed, now he goes college and shows off he's cool

But reserves his true self only for his destined princess

A round stethoscope has replaced his pencil of hopes

As his hand scripts the prescription with engrossed strokes

But no time for princess or friends who poke
As he wipes sweat and gift himself a coke

Now he hits his early 30s
Possessed with work which he calls his duty

Days and nights away …. Not for party
But to save lives …. It demands being dirty

Scalpel in hands instead of engaged ring
Curiosity for a soul mate to bring

Still trying to tie knots with the right string
Will that search be over this spring?

Forties; he now worries for his child
Will the kid be wise? Or will go wild?

Is a decision which gives headache; not mild
For which he pumps up and gets riled

Half century and now he got settled
Seen a whole lot of world as he travelled

Loads of happiness by duty which he provided

And like that, his journey of becoming a man gets completed

And hence the journey of that boy got completed as he learnt to derive his own way of living life. It's just these flash thoughts in our mind which compels us to shape ourselves. It's us who are the judge, jury and the executioner of ourselves.

To summarise...*it is these random co-incidences occuring imperfectly in our life which leads us from thoughtful morning to our journey through decades. yours might be next?*

THE END

A NOTE FOR THE READER

After reading the whole book, some grown-ups may think that the whole book is completely unnecessarily exaggerated and that, in reality, the situation is something else. But I would like to ask them, are you really sure or is it that you just know everything is alright.

Life is tough and to face the hardship one must know how to stand alone. True, but you also expect the newcomer or a teenager to learn all the things by himself. Why? Is it cheesy to talk about life or is it just that you don't want to waste your time?

Does it hold shame to ask someone what is he thinking? Is it absolutely needed that they themselves should first approach like taking an appointment? Well, am still a 20 year old and don't hold the authority to conclude, but I would be very happy if this trend of "First approach" comes to an end and that some other person in some other city in his/her bedroom thinking about all of these which I mentioned here as "imperfect co-incidences" gets his answer perfectly from someone who holds utmost value to them.

-    Author